For Anthony Aaron Mathers, who changed our lives.
And for his mother, Gynni Redmond, who changed mine.
—S. V.

For my steadfast friends: Clancy, Lily, Mama, Kiwi, Matryoshka, Tampa, and
all the other noble critters I have encountered who have made life even better.
—K. M.

SIMON & SCHUSTER BOOKS FOR YOUNG READERS • An imprint of Simon & Schuster Children's Publishing Division • 1230 Avenue of the Americas, New York, New York 10020 • Text copyright © 2020 by Susan Vaught • Illustrations copyright © 2020 by Kelly Murphy • All rights reserved, including the right of reproduction in whole or in part in any form. • SIMON & SCHUSTER BOOKS FOR YOUNG READERS is a trademark of Simon & Schuster, Inc. • For information about special discounts for bulk purchases, please contact Simon & Schuster Special Sales at 1-866-506-1949 or business@simonandschuster.com. • The Simon & Schuster Speakers Bureau can bring authors to your live event. • For more information or to book an event, contact the Simon & Schuster Speakers Bureau at 1-866-248-3049 or visit our website at www.simonspeakers.com. • Book design by Laurent Linn • The text for this book was set in Young Finesse 9. • The illustrations for this book were rendered in acrylic paints, oil paints, and gel medium on paper. • Manufactured in China • 0320 SCP • First Edition • 10 9 8 7 6 5 4 3 2 1 • Library of Congress Cataloging-in-Publication Data • Names: Vaught, Susan, author. | Murphy, Kelly, 1977- illustrator. • Title: Together we grow / written by Susan Vaught ; illustrated by Kelly Murphy. • Description: First edition. | New York : Simon & Schuster Books for Young Readers, [2020] | "A Paula Wiseman Book." | Summary: When a bad storm drives all of the farm animals into the barn, can they set aside their fears and welcome wild animals, too? • Identifiers: LCCN 2019008698| ISBN 9781534405868 (hardcover) | ISBN 9781534405875 (eBook) • Subjects: | CYAC: Stories in rhyme. | Thunderstorms—Fiction. | Domestic animals—Fiction. | Animals—Fiction. | Community life—Fiction. • Classification: LCC PZ8.3.V712564 Tog 2020 | DDC [E]—dc23 LC record available at https://lccn.loc.gov/2019008698

TOGETHER
We Grow

Written by
SUSAN VAUGHT

Illustrated by
KELLY MURPHY

A Paula Wiseman Book
SIMON & SCHUSTER BOOKS FOR YOUNG READERS
New York   London   Toronto   Sydney   New Delhi

Lightning gash!

Windy lash!

Rain and thunder,

home asunder,

Careful glances,

taking chances.

Frightened faces,

strange new places.

Paws in need,

beaks to feed.

Go away!

We're full today!

Rain-soaked, lonely.

A hope, if only . . .

Drying tears.

Calming fears.

Learn and show

together we grow.

Flat or long,

screech or song.

Slow or quick,

lumpy and slick.

Brindle and gray,

dapple or bay.

Shell and scales,

love prevails!

Large or small,

short and tall.

There is room,

there is room,

there is room . . .

for us all.